To my nephew Kevin, my mentor Deb,
and my best friend and sister Katie.

-Eric

Stay Positive,

Eric Duy

www.mascotbooks.com

Stay Positive

For more information, please contact:
Mascot Books
560 Herndon Parkway #120
Herndon, VA 20170
info@mascotbooks.com

Library of Congress Control Number: 2014921790

CPSIA Code: PRT0115A
ISBN-13: 978-1-62086-997-0

Printed in the United States

STAY POSITIVE

Eric Day
Daniel Flynn

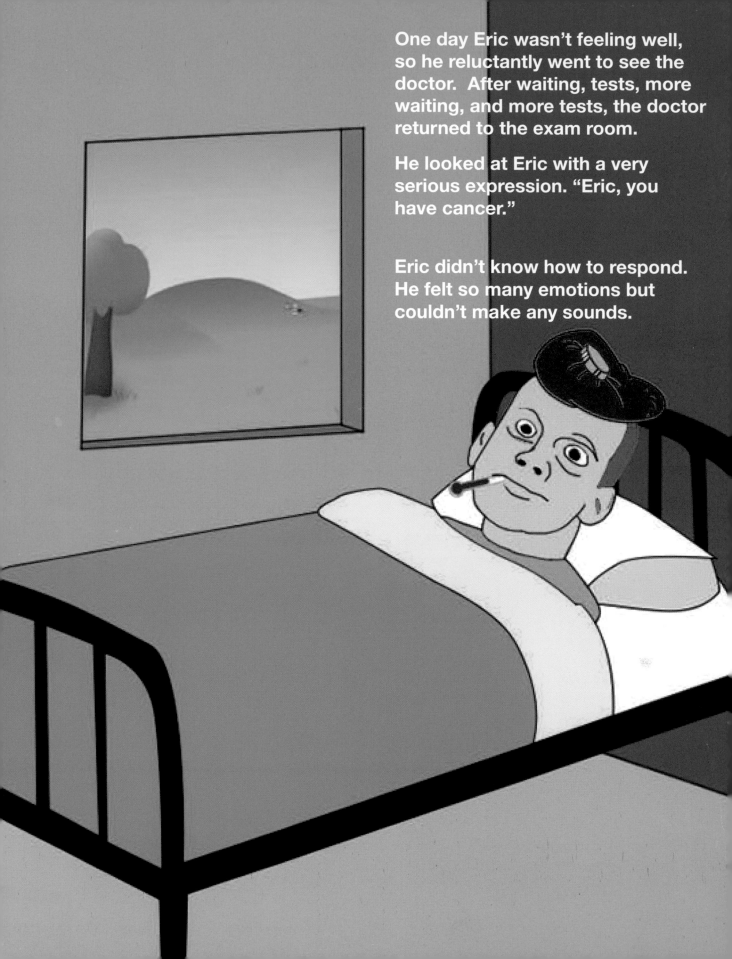

The doctor continued, "There is hope. There's a special treatment center in Bloomington, Indiana where you can get the help you need."

Eric nodded. He knew that his life would never be the same again.

The very next day, Eric and his parents arrived in Bloomington. After searching and searching for a place to stay, they decided on Jill's House.

Jill's House is a facility for people suffering from serious diseases. It is more fun than a hospital because it has a basketball hoop and a nice library with lots of books, which Eric enjoyed. The best part was Eric wasn't alone, because there were people fighting the illness just like him.

Eric was new and didn't know anyone,
so he sat alone at a table in the dining
room and picked at his food.

A little girl came over and tagged Eric, and quickly ran away. Eric, surprised, ran after her.

"What's your name?" asked Eric.

"I'm Allison and I'm six!" she replied.

"I'm Eric. Nice to meet you!"

Eric couldn't believe Allison was only six. *She must be very brave,* he thought.

Even though Eric was much older than Allison, he respected and looked up to her. Allison's illness was much more serious than Eric's, but that didn't stop her from always smiling and being happy.

Eric and Allison were eating breakfast together before their first treatment.

"Are you nervous?" asked Eric.

"Yeah," she replied. "But there's no point in being nervous. I'm trying to think of happy, positive things, like my puppy or the chocolate donut I get after treatment."

"Hey, that's great!" Eric exclaimed. "Stay positive."

"Yeah, stay positive!" Allison said.

They got up from the table and smiled at each other, remembering they had to stay positive.

During Eric's first treatment, he was very afraid. He thought of Allison and remembered he had to stay positive.

After Eric's first treatment, his headaches became very painful and he wanted to complain, but he remembered what he promised Allison.

With only one treatment a day, Eric had a lot of extra time. So he decided to teach Allison math and reading.

"What grade are you in?" asked Allison.

"I'm going to college," Eric replied.

"What's college?"

"College is a place you go after you finish high school."

Allison thought for a moment before asking, "Where is your favorite college?"

"I always dreamed about going to Butler University. It's in Indianapolis."

Eric applied to Butler, but didn't know if he would be accepted. Allison could tell Eric was happy when he talked about Butler, and she reminded him to stay positive.

Application

Sign Here_____

One day, near the end of Eric's treatments, he received a letter in the mail. He saw that it was from Butler University, and quickly went to find Allison.

His hands were shaking as he showed her the envelope.

"Stay positive!" Allison said, smiling as Eric sat down next to her.

"I got in! I got in!" he yelled. He reached out and gave Allison a big hug. "Thank you so much, Allison! If it weren't for you teaching me to stay positive, I wouldn't have even applied! I can't believe I got in!"

The last days of treatments were some of the most difficult for both Eric and Allison but they both found energy through one another. Eric knew it was going to be the hardest day of his life when he had to leave Allison. He needed her strength and courage at Butler, but no matter what, he had to stay positive.

After spending months supporting each other, Eric couldn't believe that it was time to say goodbye to Allison. He wanted to think of some way that they could keep their friendship with one another even though they would be apart.

"Got it!" he said, writing down his idea for a "Stay Positive" wristband.

When it came time to say goodbye, Eric walked up to Allison with his hands behind his back. "Hi, Allison," he smiled, as she finished packing her belongings into a suitcase.

"Eric!" She ran over and gave him a hug. "I'm so happy to finally be going home. But I'll miss you." She squeezed him tighter.

Eric showed Allison what he had in his hands. "We just have to stay positive," He slipped the wristband onto Allison's arm. "Thank you for teaching me that we can get through this if we just stay positive."

Allison smiled, "Thank you!" she said as she gave Eric a big hug.

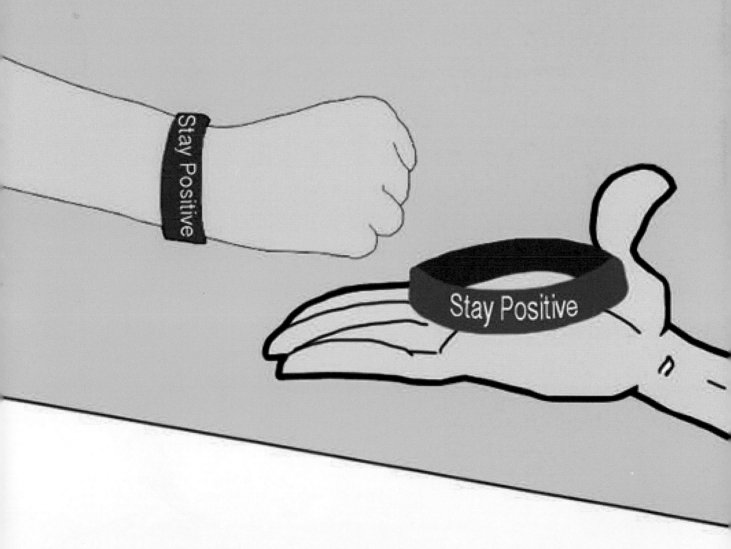

Eric walked back up to his room and started packing up his things. He was surprised to realize the two months he spent with Allison were the best of his life. Allison helped Eric learn no matter what life throws at you, the only thing you can control is your attitude. *Stay positive,* he thought to himself, as he smiled.

After leaving Jill's House, Eric worked to adjust to normal life before heading off to Butler University. When he arrived at school, he was nervous. He didn't know what to do or where to go. Before he panicked, he looked down at his wrist and saw those two simple words, "Stay Positive."

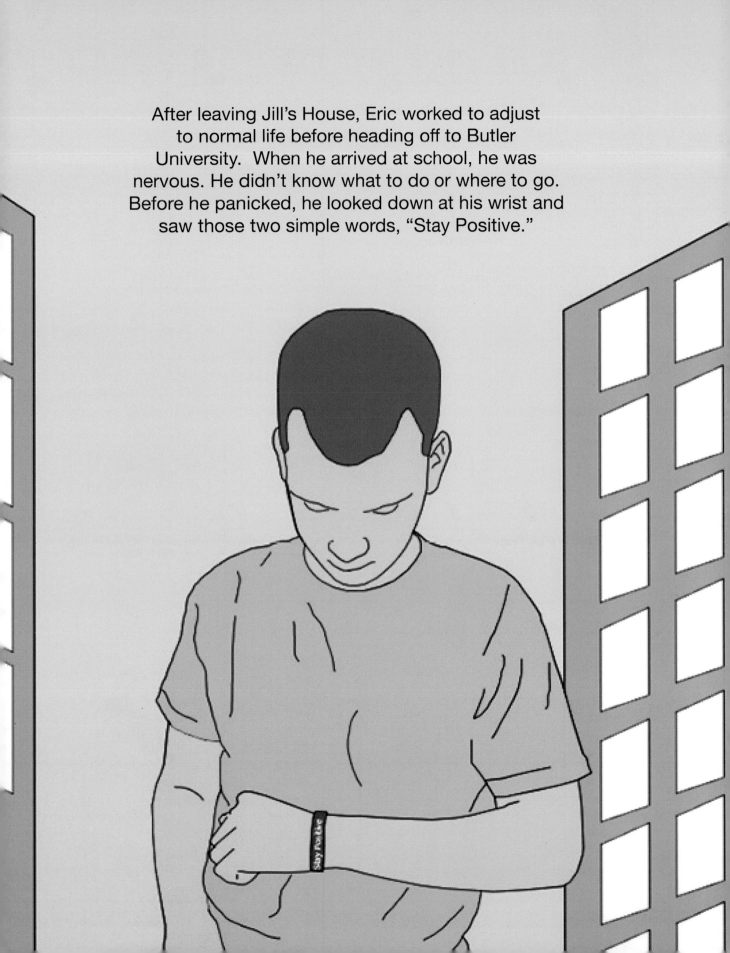

Eric arrived at Butler University and went to his dorm room to start unpacking. As he started putting away his clothes, someone walked into the room.

"Hi, I'm Bo. I guess we're roommates."

"I'm Eric. Nice to meet you."

"What's that on your wrist?" Bo asked.

Eric smiled at the thought of Allison. "It's a long story. But I'll tell you about it if you give me a hand with unpacking."

Bo and Eric became great friends, and Bo loved hearing the story about Allison.

"I should remember to stay positive, too," he said.
"Any chance I can also have a wristband?"

Eric had fifty wristbands to give away. After Eric gave that first wristband away, everyone on campus wanted one, Eric started to sell them.

Instead of keeping the money, Eric and Allison decided to donate the money to the Jill's House and cancer research. As time went on, the wristbands became popular all over the United States! Now, there is at least one wristband in each of the fifty states!

It doesn't matter how old you are, where you come from, or what your story may be; with a positive attitude, you can change the world, one person at a time.

As you move forward with your life, Eric and Allison want to remind you that no matter what happens...

Thanks you for your donations for the creation of this book and your continued support of *Stay Positive*.

Sarah Bakian
Colin Brown
Bob & Jennifer Caban
Carl & Mary Alice Chrabascz
Dayna Culp
Bo Davidson
Ron & Lori Day
Dick & Martha Day
Susan Debkowski-Wilson
Steve & Lisa Farley
Seth & Lauren Ferguson
Tom & Kelsey Flynn
ABCD Guth
Erin Houser
Tammy Johnson
Bob Jones
Mary Kaufman
Mike & Deb Lecklider
Linda Leasure
Beverley McDonald
Deborah & Delanie Olsen
Josh Patrick
Jay & Mindy Potter
Woody & Sherry Schinbeckler
Lori Showley
Trudy Southe
Ryan & Shelly Welch
Bob Zeronik

About the Author

Eric is from Plymouth, Indiana. When he isn't working on Stay Positive, he loves watching the Minnesota Vikings and the Butler Bulldogs, his two favorite sports teams. He enjoys traveling across the country with his parents, Ron and Lori, along with his sister, Katie, and his brother-in-law, Brendan. In 2014, Eric was given the "Leader of the Year" award from the College of Communications at Butler. The award is given to one Butler student for their impact and innovation towards the community. Eric still stays in contact with his little friend, Allison. She is currently starting third grade.

You can contact Eric by email at
staypositivebandsG3@gmail.com
staypositivebands.org